WHERE'S MY TRACTOR? LOL [OUT LOUD] OR JOKES FROM THE HERB GARDEN:

A Collection of Jokes, Puns, Humor, and Words of Wisdom

by

Herbert Lindsey

DORRANCE PUBLISHING CO
EST. 1920
PITTSBURGH, PENNSYLVANIA 15238

Dorrance Publishing Co
585 Alpha Drive
Pittsburgh, PA 15238
Visit our website at www.dorrancebookstore.com

ISBN: 979-8-88729-291-5
eISBN: 979-8-88729-791-0

JOKES

A ventriloquist is performing with his dummy on his lap. He's telling a dumb-blonde joke when a young platinum haired beauty jumps to her feet.

"What gives you the right to stereotype blondes that way?" she shouts. "What does hair color have to do with my worth as a human being?"

Flustered, the ventriloquist begins to stammer out an apology.

"You keep out of this!" she yells. "I'm talking to that little jerk on your knee."

Every ten years, the monks in the monastery are allowed to break their vow of silence to speak two words. Ten years go by and it's one monk's first chance to speak. He thinks for a second before saying, "Food bad."

Ten years later he says, "Bed hard."

It's the big day, a decade later. He gives the head monk a long stare and says, "I quit."

"I'm not surprised," the head monk says, "you've done nothing but complain since you got here."

Leaving a funeral, my 13-year-old son dropped a heavy question on me: "What will happen to us if you and dad die?"

My young daughter piped up with the answer, "We'd go in the limo."

A guy spots a sign outside a house that reads: Talking Dog for Sale. Intrigued, he walks in.

"So, what have you done with your life?" he asks the dog.

"I've led a very full life," says the dog. "I lived in the Alps rescuing avalanche victims. Then, I served my country in Iraq, and now I spend my days reading to the residents of a retirement home."

The guy is flabbergasted. He asks the dog's owner, "Why on earth would you want to get rid of an incredible dog like that?"

The owner says, "Because he's a liar! He never did any of that."

Two hunters are out in the woods when one of them collapses. He's not breathing and his eyes are glazed. The other guy whips out his cell phone and calls 911.

"I think my friend is dead!" he yells. "What can I do?"

The operator says, "Calm down. First, let's make sure he's dead."

There's a silence, then a gunshot.

Back on the phone the guy says, "Okay, now what?"

A turtle is crossing the road when he's mugged by two snails. When the police show up, they ask him what happened.

The shaken turtle replies, "I don't know. It all happened so fast."

A man is walking in a graveyard when he hears the third symphony played backward. When it's over, the second symphony starts, also backwards and then the first.

"What's going on?" he asks a cemetery worker.

"It's Beethoven," says the worker. "He's decomposing."

A poodle and a collie are walking together when the poodle suddenly unloads on his friend. "My life is a mess," he says. "My owner is mean. My girlfriend ran away with a schnauzer and I'm as jittery as a cat."

"Why don't you go see a psychiatrist?" asks the collie.

"I can't," says the poodle. "I'm not allowed on the couch."

An older couple is discussing the inevitable matter of death.

The wife asks her husband, "If I die before you do, will you remarry?"

To which the husband replies, "Well, I don't want to be lonely for the rest of my life, so yes." The wife then asks, "What about the house? Will you live in the same place?"

The husband says, "Well, I suppose, I mean, it's already paid for."

The wife, getting a little protective, asks, "And what about my car?"

Again, the husband says, "Well, it's already paid for."

The wife, annoyed at this point, shouts, "What about my golf clubs!?"

To which he husband replies, "Oh, no, she's left-handed."

I was at my desk at our Coast Guard base while another guardsman waited for a fax to come in. Once it arrived, he stared incredulously at the blank piece of paper.

"Can I borrow your phone?" he asked. "I need to call these people and let them know their fax machine is out of ink."

When a fellow Army ROTC cadet was kept out of Airbourne school because of poor grades, his grandfather was confused.

"Wait a minute," he said to his grandson. "You're telling me that these days you have to be smart to jump out of an airplane?"

To show his appreciation to the community, our base commanding officer held an open house which included a free meal. I was busing tables when I noticed a family leaving a large tip. "Excuse me, we can't accept tips," I told them.

"It's not for you," said the woman. "That's to help send your chef to culinary school."

"What's wrong, Officer?" I asked the cop those three dreaded words seconds after he'd pulled me over.

"Didn't you notice you were driving the wrong way down a one-way street?" he asked.

"No," I said. "I turned on this street from Maple, and there were no signs indicating this was a one-way street."

"That's because you were going the wrong way down Maple, too."

As I pulled into a crowded parking lot, I asked the cop who was standing there, "Is it alright to park here?"

"No," he said. "Can't you see that No Parking sign?"

"What about all these other cars parked here?"

He shrugged. "They didn't ask."

I'd had enough of searching high and low for my newspaper every morning, so I called the delivery service and complained.

After listening to my complaint, the clerk asked, "Where do you usually find your paper?" "Sometimes in the bushes and sometimes on my front porch," I stated.

"Okay," she said. "And where would you prefer to find it?"

After not having fired a gun in years, I visited a nearby pistol range. I was awful and couldn't hit a thing. Turning to my friend who was watching I said, "You know, it may be hard to believe, but I was on my school's shooting team."

He asked, "What were you... the target?"

The medical clinic I worked for sent patients a letter asking if they needed transportation to appointments and if so, why? Here are some of their responses:

- I am under the doctor and cannot breathe.
- My husband is dead and will not bring me.
- I cannot walk uphill unless it is down, and the hill to your clinic is up.

Three days of suffering through a nasty virus left me wiped out, but I found a silver lining on the very first day I crawled out of bed. Throwing on a pair of pants, I called out to my husband, "Look! These jeans fit! They finally fit!"

"Great," he said. "But those are my jeans."

My current wife and my ex-wife rarely talk, but they were thrown together when my mother-in-law had all of the grandkids to her home for a cookout. Luckily, I wasn't there, which irked my ex.

"Where's Paul?" she asked.

"He's home mowing the lawn," said my wife.

My ex smiled. "I wish I'd married someone like that."

Visiting family in Kentucky is a heart-stopping experience if only because my brother-in-law drives in the middle of the road, straddling the double lines that separate traffic. My sister-in-law does little to ease my fears. Seeing the horror in my eyes, she once said, "Don't worry, everyone around here drives in the middle of the road."

A man went to a job interview. His resume was fantastic and his qualities made him a perfect fit for the company. The interviewers were very impressed.

"You're a strong candidate and we would like to hire you, however, there's this five-year gap in your resume. What were you doing during that time?'

"I went to Yale."

"Wow, great! You're hired."

"Yay, I've got a yob!'

Q: What did the farmer say when he couldn't find his tractor?

A: Where's my tractor?

A man is trying on shoes.

The salesman asks, "So, how do they feel?"

"They're a little too tight," the man replies.

"Well, try pulling the tongue out," the clerk suggests.

"Okay," he says, "They thill theel a bith thoo thight."

My wife asked me, "If you won the lottery would you still love me?"

"Of course, I would. I'd miss you but I'd still love you."

A man speaks frantically into the phone, "My wife is pregnant, and her contractions are only two minutes apart!"

The doctor asks, "Is this her first child?"

"No, you idiot," the man shouts, "this is her husband!"

When my wife told me to stop impersonating a flamingo, I had to put my foot down.

Our base's Army Exchange service carried a particular brand of deodorant that I liked and bought for years. Then one day I couldn't find it. I asked an employee whether they still carried my deodorant.

"No, we don't," she said. "It was always selling out and I could never keep it in stock, so I quit ordering it."

A coach walks into the locker room before a game, looks over at his star player and says, "I'm not supposed to play you since you failed math, but we need you in there, so what I have to do is ask you a math question and if you get it right, you can play."

The player agrees and the coach looks intently into his eyes and says, "Okay, now concentrate, what is two plus two?"

The player thinks for a minute and answers, "Four?"

"Did you say four?" the coach exclaims.

At that, all of the other players on the team start yelling, "Come on, coach, give him another chance."

Lamar is out with his friends and stops by his grandmother's home for a visit. There's a bowl of peanuts on the coffee table and Lamar and his friends start snacking on them.

Before they leave, one friend says, "Nice to meet you, ma'am, and thank you for the peanuts." "You're welcome," grandmother says, "Ever since I lost my dentures, all I can do is suck the chocolate off of them."

Why did the kid have string beans stuck up his nose? He wasn't eating right.

A man goes to the doctor and says, "Doctor, wherever I touch, it hurts."

"What do you mean?" the doctor asks.

"When I touch my shoulder, it hurts. If I touch my knee...ouch! When I touch my forehead, it really, really hurts."

"I know what's wrong with you," the doctor says. "You've broken your finger."

On a fishing trip to a remote lake in northern Quebec, I asked the outfitter, "Do you stay here during the winter?"

"No," he said. "The snow gets too deep. We can't get supplies in, so like many Canadians, I go south for the winter."

"Oh," I asked. "Where do you go?"

"Vermont."

After I had paid for my items in an adorable Italian shop, the salesperson said, "*Grazie,*" which is Italian for thank you. My Italian isn't too good, but I remembered that the Italian word for you're welcome was the same as the name of a popular American spaghetti sauce, so I confidently replied, "Ragu!" and walked out of the store. A few blocks later, it hit me: I had the wrong spaghetti sauce. You're welcome in Italian is Prego.

What is brown and sticky? A stick!!!

A man walks into a library and orders a hamburger.

The librarian says, "Sir, this is a library."

The man apologizes and whispers, "I'd like a hamburger, please."

A husband and wife, who own a circus, walk into an adoption agency looking to adopt a child. "Are you sure the circus is the best place for a child?" asked the social worker. "I mean, all those dangerous animals and the constant traveling?"

"The animals are trained," says the wife, "And we have a state-of-the-art, 55-foot motor home that is equipped with a large nursery."

"How will you educate the child?"

"We've arranged for a full-time tutor to teach all the regular subjects, as well as Mandarin and computer programming." explained the husband.

"And the nanny is certified in pediatric care, child welfare and nutrition," the wife added.

The social worker is impressed. "Well, you do seem perfect. What age were you looking to adopt?"

The husband replies, "It doesn't matter, as long as they fit into the cannon."

A string walks into a bar with a few friends and orders a beer.

The bartender says, "I'm sorry, but we don't serve strings here."

The string goes back to his table, ties himself into a loop and messes up his hair. He walks back to the bar and orders a beer.

The bartender squints at him and says, "Hey, aren't you a string?"

To which the string says, "Nope, I'm a frayed knot."

A widower and a widow attend their 70th class reunion and a long-ago spark is rekindled.

At the end of the night, he asks, "Will you marry me?"

"Yes, yes, I will," she says enthusiastically.

The next morning, the widower wakes up troubled. Confused, he calls and asks, "Did you say yes or no to marrying me?"

"I said yes, and I'm glad you called because I couldn't remember who asked me."

A skeleton goes into a bar and climbs onto a stool.

The bartender asks, "May I help you, sir?"

"Yes," says the skeleton, "Bring me a beer… and a mop."

When I was a boy, I had a disease that required me to eat dirt three times a day in order to survive. It's a good thing my older brother told me about it.

Eddy Money's wife said to him, "You look heavy on TV."

"Honey, the camera adds ten pounds."

She asked, "Well, how many cameras did they use?"

Something tells me I need to lose some weight. During a recent trip to visit my son and his family, I stopped off at a bakery to pick up a dessert. After scanning the display, I settled on a dozen pound-cake cupcakes.

The clerk's response: "Will that be for here or to go?"

The police arrested a man selling secret formula tablets he claimed gave eternal life. It was actually the fifth time he'd been caught for committing the same medical fraud. He'd been arrested in 1794, 1856, 1928 and 1983.

My wife cooks for me like I'm a god by placing burnt offerings before me every night.

I told my wife I wanted to be cremated. She made an appointment for me next Tuesday!

Two old guys, Fred and Sam, went to the movies. A few minutes into the film, Fred notices Sam searching for something under the seat.

"What are you doing?" Fred asked.

"Well," Sam said with aggravation, "I had a candy in my mouth, but it fell out."

"Forget it. It'll be dirty now."

"I've got to find it. My teeth are in it."

It always irked my single mother that her grocery store didn't carry eggs in packages of six. They only came by the dozen. Then, one day, her wish came true. She walked into the grocery and found fresh eggs in cartons of six.

"I was so excited," she told us later, "I bought two cartons."

I can give you the cause of anaphylactic shock in a nutshell.

My wife does this cute thing now and then where she goes out and shops for next year's yard sale items.

One of the world's strongest man events should be pulling apart two shopping carts that are stuck together.

I picked up a hitchhiker. He seemed like a nice guy. After a few miles, he asked if I was afraid that he might be a serial killer? I told him the odds of two serial killers being in the same car were extremely unlikely.

I tried to have my mother's landline disconnected, but the customer service representative told me that since the phone was in my father's name, he'd have to be the one to put in the request. The fact that he'd been dead for forty years didn't sway her.

Then a solution hit me, "If I stop paying the bill, you can turn off the service, right?"

"Well, yes," she said reluctantly, "but that would ruin his credit."

I couldn't figure out why the baseball was getting bigger. Then it hit me.

It was so cold in D.C. today, I saw a politician with his hands in his own pockets.

What's orange and sounds like a parrot? A carrot!

My boss just texted me: "Send me one of your funny jokes."

I texted him back: "I'm busy working, I'll send you one later."

"That's hilarious," he texted. "Send another one."

Never criticize someone until you have walked a mile in their shoes. That way, when you criticize them, you'll be a mile away and you'll have their shoes.

A kindergarten teacher was telling her students about different kinds of animals. "Whales are the largest," she said, "but they cannot swallow people because their throats are too small."

"But in the Bible, it says Jonah was swallowed by a whale," said a little girl.

"You can't always believe what you read," replied the teacher.

"Well, when I go to heaven," said the little girl, "I'll ask Jonah."

"And if Jonah didn't go to heaven?" the teacher asked.

"Well, then, you can ask him."

A man walks into a rooftop bar and takes a seat next to another guy.

"What are you drinking?" he asks.

"Magic beer," his neighbor replies.

"Oh, yeah? What's so magic about it?"

He swigs some beer, dives off the roof, flies around the building and finally returns to his seat with a triumphant smile.

"Amazing," the man says. "Lemme try some of that." The man grabs the beer, downs a big swallow, leaps off the roof and plummets fifteen stories to his death.

The bartender shakes his head. "You know, you're a real jerk when you're drunk, Superman."

I was playing chess with my friend and he said, "Let's make this interesting," so we stopped playing.

When I read about the evils of drinking, I gave up reading.

My doctor gave me six months to live, but when I couldn't pay the bill, he gave me six months more.

I haven't reported my stolen credit card to the police because whoever stole it is spending less than my wife.

I wondered why I was putting on a few extra pounds without increasing my calorie intake and then I discovered why. When I was shampooing my hair, I was, of course, letting the water run down my body. Printed very plainly on the label of the shampoo bottle is this warning: For extra body and volume.

I am now washing my hair with Dawn dishwashing soap whose label proclaims: Dissolves fat that is otherwise difficult to remove.

If I don't answer the phone, you'll know I'm in the shower.

At the supermarket, a customer buying a lot of groceries was checking out. As the clerk lifted the final bag, its bottom gave out, sending the contents crashing to the floor.

"They don't make these bags like they used to," the clerk said to the customer. "That was supposed to happen in your driveway."

For weeks I've been telling him not to buy anything for my birthday, and he still forgot to bring me anything.

My doctor told me to stop having intimate dinners for four, unless there were three other people.

My grandfather is a little forgetful, but he likes to give me advice. One day he took me aside and left me there.

Three brothers ages 92, 94 and 96, respectively, live together in a house. One night the 96-year-old draws a bath, puts his foot in and hesitates. He yells down the stairs, "Was I getting into or out of the bath?"

The 94-year-old yells back, "I don't know. I'll come up and see." He starts up the stairs and pauses, then yells, "Was I going up the stairs or coming down?"

The 92-year-old was sitting at the kitchen table having coffee and listening to his brothers. He shakes his head and mutters, "I sure hope I never get that forgetful."

He knocks on wood for good luck, then yells, "I'll come up and help both of you as soon as I see who's at the door."

Guys have feelings too, but like, who cares?

You are over the hill when your knees buckle but your belt won't.

There are three things men can't say: I'm wrong, I'm lost, and I can't fix it.

If you don't have anything good to say about anyone, come sit by me.

There are three basic food groups: canned, frozen, and take-out.

Which rock group has four guys who can neither play nor sing? Mount Rushmore.

What do Alexander the Great and Winnie the Pooh have in common? The same middle name.

If you ever get cold, go stand in the corner of the room for a while. They're usually 90 degrees.

My last New Year's resolution was to lose ten pounds. I missed it by 15 pounds.

My wife has a slight impediment of speech. Every now and then she has to stop to breathe.

Somebody complimented me on my driving today. They left a note on my windshield that said: PARKING FINE.

A son said to his father, "I'll be good if you pay me a dollar."
    The father replied rather sternly, "Why son, when I was your age, I was good for nothing."

Buddha didn't get married because his wife would have said, "What, are you just going to sit around like that all day?"

The biggest seller is cookbooks and the second is diet books. How not to eat what you've just learned to cook?

Give a man a fish and he will eat for a day. Teach him to fish, and he will sit in a boat and drink beer all day.

My grandmother is over eighty and still doesn't need glasses. She drinks right out of the bottle.

I sold my house this week. I got a pretty good price for it, but it made my landlord very angry.

We owe a lot to Thomas Edison, if it weren't for him, we'd be watching television by candlelight.

A moose is an animal with horns on the front of his head and a hunting lodge wall on the back of it.

Two couples were taking an evening walk, the men were in front with their wives following behind. One of the men was telling his friend about a restaurant, but he could not remember the name of it.

He asked his friend, "What's the name of that flower that is red and has thorns?"

His friend replied, "A rose."

He then turned and called out to his wife, "Hey, Rose, what's the name of that restaurant we were eating at tonight?"

I remember when the candle shop burned down. Everyone stood around and sang happy birthday.

I'm into golf now. I'm getting pretty good. I can almost hit the ball as far as I can throw the clubs.

My mother said, "You won't amount to anything because you procrastinate."

I said, "You just wait."

We need a twelve-step program for compulsive talkers. They could call it, On-Anon-Anon.

PUNS

When I moved into my new igloo, my friends threw me a surprise housewarming party. Now I'm homeless.

We have a horse, we call him Mayo, sometimes Mayo neighs.

Is it true that the inventor of diapers keeps getting a little behind in his work?

I went down to the paint store to get thinner. It didn't work.

Breaking news: Snap, Crackle and Pop Murdered! Cereal killer sought by police.

If you go to a plastic surgeon to get rhinoplasty, you get to pick your own nose.

I accidently got catsup in my eyes. Now, I have Heinz sight.

He threw sodium chloride at me! That's a salt.

Fried chicken tasted terrible in Aristotle's time because it was fried in ancient Greece.

Thanks for teaching me the meaning of plethora. It means a lot.

I love the way the earth rotates. It really makes my day.

I thought the dryer was shrinking my clothes. Turns out it was the refrigerator.

We've heard about Newton discovering gravity when an apple fell on his head, but when did he discover the fig?

I have a really flat tummy. That's flat with a silent L.

Australia's biggest export is boomerangs. It's also their biggest import.

Yesterday, I swallowed some food coloring. I feel like I dyed a little inside.

You've heard of Murphy's Law? Well, here's Cole's Law: Mix carrots, cabbage, and mayonnaise.

I knew a woman who owned a taser. She was stunning.

A huge stack of toilet paper fell on me in the supermarket. I'm okay though, just soft tissue damage.

When one door closes, another one opens. Other than that, it's a pretty good car.

I'm very nervous about my final exams in Math. I think my chances of passing are about 40/40.

Irony is the opposite of wrinkly.

Well, to be Frank, I'd have to change my name.

Electricians have to strip to make ends meet.

A cow stumbles into a pot field. Steaks have never been higher.

He who laughs last didn't get it.

Definition of retired: I was tired yesterday and I'm tired again today.

Broken puppets for sale—No strings attached.

Inspecting mirrors is something I could see myself doing.

No matter how far you push the envelope, it will still be stationary.

How do you kill a circus? Go for the juggler.

What do you call a piece of toast at a zoo? Bread in captivity.

I wanted to buy a camouflage shirt, but I didn't see one.

Once you've seen a shopping center, you've seen a mall.

When you swim in a creek and an eel bites your cheek, that's a moray.

If a drummer comes out of retirement will there be serious repercussions?

The guy at the furniture store told me the sofa would seat five people without any problems. Then it occurred to me, I don't know five people without any problems.

Woman: Do men still open car doors?
    Man: How do you think they get inside?

2020: If your car is running, I'm voting for it.

What happens if you get scared half to death twice?

This is my stepladder. I never knew my real ladder.

I checked myself into the Hokey Pokey Clinic and I turned myself around.

Is there ever a day when there isn't a mattress sale?

I'm opening a chain of Elvis themed restaurants. It will be for people who love meat tender.

NEWSPAPER HEADLINES

Astronaut takes blame for gas in space craft

Reagan wins on budget, but more lies ahead

Iraqi head seeks arms

One-armed man applauds kindness of strangers

Two Soviet ships collide, one dies

Miner refuses to work after death

Joint committee investigates marijuana use

Prostitutes appeal to Pope

Police begin campaign to run down jaywalkers

New study of obesity looks for larger test group

Blind woman gets new kidney from dad she hasn't seen in years

Statistics show teen pregnancy drops off significantly after age twenty-five

Skywalkers in Korea cross Han solo

Federal agents raid gun shop, find weapons

Two sisters reunited after eighteen years at checkout counter

War dims hope for peace

Argyle socked by tornado

EPITAPHS AND EPITHETS

In a New Mexico Cemetery:

HERE LIES JOHNNY YEAST, PARDON ME FOR NOT RISING

A lawyer's epitaph in England:

SIR JOHN STRANGE, HERE LIES AN HONEST LAWYER, AND THAT IS STRANGE

From Margaret Daniels' grave in Virginia:

SHE ALWAYS SAID HER FEET WERE KILLING HER, BUT NOBODY BELIEVED HER

Winston Churchill:

I AM READY TO MEET MY MAKER: WHETHER MY MAKER IS PREPARED FOR THE GREAT ORDEAL OF MEETING ME IS ANOTHER MATTER

From a grave in Nova Scotia:

HERE LIES EZEKIAL AIKLE, AGE 102, THE GOOD DIE YOUNG

British Cemetery, 1767

HERE LIES ANN MANN, WHO LIVED AN OLD MAID BUT DIED AN OLD MANN

Mel Blanc's epitaph:
THAT'S ALL FOLKS

On the gravestone of Harry Edsel Smith of Albany, New York:
BORN 1903-DIED 1942 LOOKED UP THE ELEVATOR SHAFT TO SEE IF THE ELEVATOR WAS ON THE WAY DOWN. IT WAS.

H.G. Wells epitaph/epithet:
I TOLD YOU, YOU DARNED FOOLS

Jedediah Goodwin, Auctioneer born 1828:
GOING! GOING! GONE, 1876

From a Burlington, Vermont headstone:
SHE LIVED WITH HER HUSBAND FIFTY YEARS AND DIED IN THE CONFIDENT HOPE OF A BETTER LIFE

Studs Terkel:
CURIOSITY DID NOT KILL THIS CAT

Epitaph of a Rhode Island fisherman:
CAPTAIN THOMAS COFFIN. DIED 1842. AGE 50 YEARS. HE'S DONE-A-CATCHING COD AND GONE TO MEET HIS GOD.

From a Maryland Cemetery:
HERE LIES AN ATHEIST. ALL DRESSED UP AND NOWHERE TO GO.

From a Vermont Cemetery:
SACRED TO THE MEMORY OF MY HUSBAND, JOHN BARNES, WHO DIED JANUARY 3, 1803. HIS COMELY YOUNG WIDOW, AGED 23, HAS MANY QUALIFICATIONS OF A GOOD WIFE, AND YEARNS TO BE COMFORTED.

Epitaph of an adulterous husband in Atlanta:

GONE BUT NOT FORGIVEN

HERE LIES PA

PA LIKED WIMMIN

MA CAUGHT PA WITH TWO SWIMMIN

HERE LIES PA

WORDS OF WISDOM

One of the very best rules of conversation is to never say anything which any of the company wish had been left unsaid.

Jonathan Swift

It is only necessary to grow old to become more charitable and even indulgent. I see no fault committed by others that I have not committed myself.

Johann Wolfgang Von Goethe

Kindness is more than deeds. It is an attitude, an expression, a look, a touch. It is anything that lifts another person.

C. Neil Trait

Where is Hollywood located? Chiefly between the ears, in that part of the American brain lately vacated by God.

Erica Jong

Restraint and discipline and examples of virtue and justice, these are the things that form the education of the world.

Edmund Burke

To keep your marriage brimming with love in the loving cup, whenever you're wrong admit it; whenever you're right, shut up.

Ogden Nash

Don't tell your problems to people, eighty percent don't care, and the other twenty percent are glad you have them.

Lou Holtz

Even the rich are hungry for love, for being cared for, for being wanted, for having someone to call their own.

Mother Teresa

I find television very educational. Every time someone switches it on, I go into another room and read a good book.

Groucho Marx

Non-violence is not a garment to be put on and off at will. Its seat is in the heart, and it must be an inseparable part of our being.

Mahatma Gandhi

When a girl marries, she exchanges the attention of all the other men of her acquaintance for the inattention of just one.

Helen Rowland

Associate yourself with men of good quality if you esteem your own reputation. It is better to be alone than in bad company.

George Washington

The beauty that addresses itself to the eyes is only the spell of the moment; the eye of the body is not always that of the soul.

George Sand

If you go looking for a friend, you're going to find they're scarce. If you go out to be a friend, you'll find them everywhere.

Zig Ziglar

Education is the ability to listen to almost anything without losing your temper or your self-confidence.

Robert Frost

The minute a phrase becomes current, it becomes an apology for not thinking accurately to the end of the sentence.

Oliver Wendell Holmes

There is a great difference between knowing and understanding; you can know a lot about something and not really understand it.

Charles Kettering

The liberty of the individual is no gift of civilization. It was greatest before there was any civilization.

Sigmund Freud

There are few people so stubborn in their atheism who when danger is pressing in will not acknowledge the divine power.

Plato

In a controversy, the instant we feel anger, we have already ceased striving for the truth and have begun striving for ourselves.

Thomas Carlyle

Money is like love; it kills slowly and painfully the one who withholds it, and enlivens the other who turns it on his fellowman.

Kahlil Gibson

Mortality is not the doctrine of how we make ourselves happy, but how we may make ourselves worthy of happiness.

Immanuel Kant

No people is wholly civilized where a distinction is drawn between stealing an office and stealing a purse.

Theodore Roosevelt

We deem those happy who from the experience of life have learnt to bear its ills without being overcome by them.

Carl Jong

A doctrine serves no purpose in itself, but it is indispensable to live one if only to avoid being deceived by false doctrine.

Simms Weil

Kindness in words creates confident, kindness in thinking creates profoundness, kindness in giving creates love.

Lao Tzu

Sticks and stones are hard on bones aimed with angry art. Words can sting like anything but silence breaks the heart.

Phyllis McGinley

Fame comes with its own standard, a guy who twitches is just another guy with a twitch – unless he's Humphrey Bogart.

Sammy Davis Jr.

Married couples resemble a pair of scissors, often moving in opposite directions, yet punishing anyone who gets between them.

Sydney Smith

I count him braver who overcomes his desires than him who conquers his enemies, for the hardest victory is over self.

Aristotle

In general, mankind, since the improvement of cockery eats twice as much as nature requires.

Benjamin Franklin